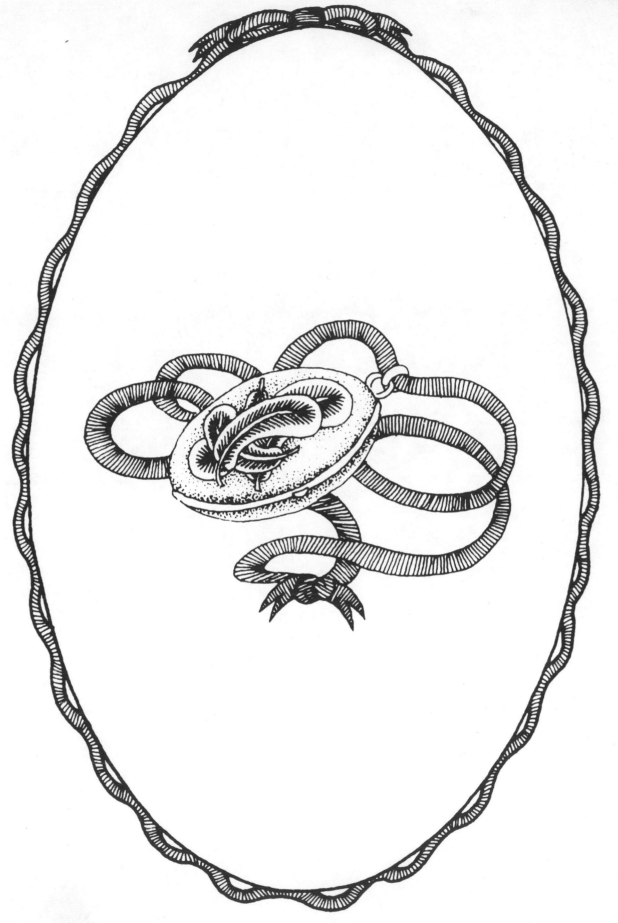

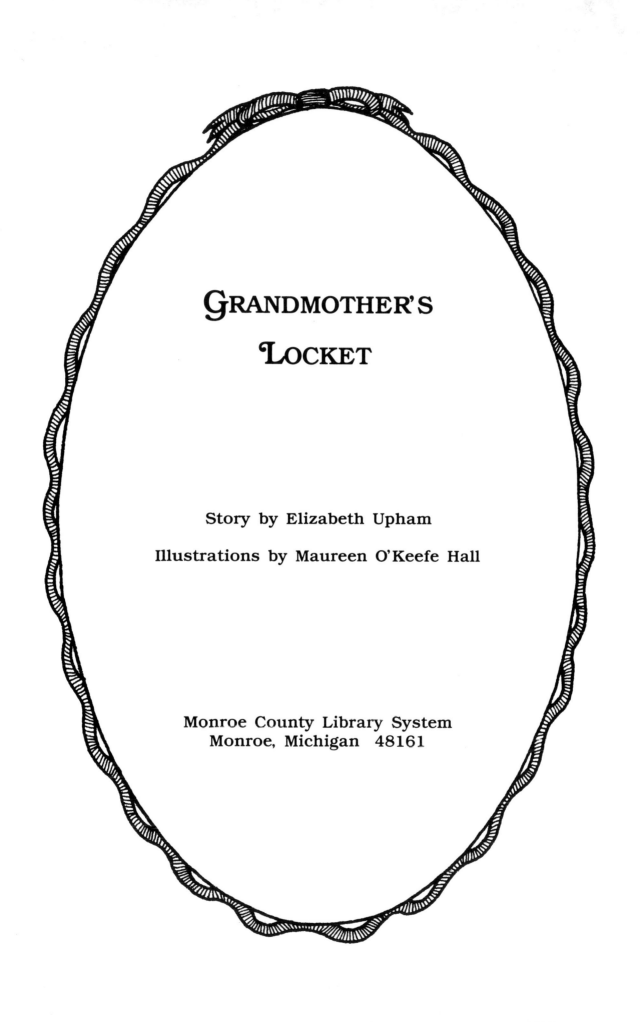

GRANDMOTHER'S LOCKET

Story by Elizabeth Upham

Illustrations by Maureen O'Keefe Hall

Monroe County Library System
Monroe, Michigan 48161

Dedicated To

Clara

"What do you want to do, Maia?"

"I don't know. What do you want to do?"

"We could play dress-up on the porch."

"Dress-up's no fun any more. How about climbing the tree in the school-yard to see the nest the robin left?"

"I can't climb in my new jeans, but we could ride bikes."

"There's only one. Let's go in my room and read books."

"Remember? Your mom said we had to stay outside until Lacey wakes up from her nap."

"Oh, yeah."

"Come on, Maia, we've got the whole day. Let's think of something good!"

"Okay... I know!! We could go visit Aunt Bett!"

"Who's Aunt Bett?"

1

"She's the neatest lady! She likes kids a lot and she tells us stories.
Lets go!"

"All right!"

"Do you think she's home?"

"We'll find out. Wait till you see her Little Brown Bear room. You've
never seen anything like it! Bears, dolls, toys and books everywhere!"

"Let's knock."

"Hi Aunt Bett! This is my cousin Jessica. Could you tell us a story?"

"Hello Maia. I'm glad to make your acquaintance, Jessica. I'll introduce
you to Kitty Gray and Charlie and..."

"Grrrrr... Rowf! Rowf! Grrowf!"

"Now Mr. Tibbs, you behave yourself. That's not how to win friends and
influence people. Jessica, you'll have to excuse Tibby. When he was a
puppy, before we got him from the Humane Society, someone used to hit

him. When anyone puts a hand down to pet him, he thinks he's going to get hit. But you're a good dog, aren't you Mr. Tibbs? Here's a biscuit. Now you go lay down and be a good dog."

"You have such pretty cats, Aunt Bett. Charlie is black and white like my cat at home."

"Thank you Jessica. Now let me see, what story could I tell you?"

"Let's have some cookies and milk and I'll tell you a story an old friend of mine told me. Would you like that?"

"We sure would. Who was your friend?"

"Well, her name was Gustie and when she was a little girl she used to live in Germany. She told me many things about life in Germany, but I'll tell you this one because it begins in autumn, and it is autumn now. Let's see, I suppose that Gustie was about eight or nine when this story begins, just your age.

One hundred years ago, in a little German village there lived a family named "Dubrect." The children's names were Gustie (for Gustava) and Karl. Gustie and Karl were good children (and good friends also).

At the end of each summer, the herdsmen would lead their flocks down from the hills and mountainsides into the villages. There the women of the households would choose the animals their family would need for food during the long winter.

Mrs. Dubrect chose goats for milk, cheese and butter and some sheep for wool to make sweaters and such. Some of these sheep would also be used for food. Finally, she chose some fine young geese, one of which she had planned to fatten for Christmas dinner!

Gustie and Karl were with Mrs. Dubrect that day. They immediately fell in love with one of the geese. This goose was diffcrent from the others. She seemed to understand them. She didn't bite like the others. She was considerate and so polite that she stood quietly and didn't honk unless spoken to! Gustie and Karl named their goose "Wilhelmina." Wilhelmina came when they called her and her pretty eyes sparkled with love!

The children took such good care of her. They fed her with crusts from their own bread, made her a bed by the fire and took her everywhere they went.

One morning Mrs. Dubrect told the children not to get too attached to Wilhelmina because she was the goose the family would have for Christmas dinner. Oh, were Gustie and Karl dismayed! They spent their days thinking of ways to keep Wilhelmina safe.

They prayed at night that they would be able to think of something soon.

The days passed into weeks, and weeks into months, until it was only two days until Christmas. Gustie and Karl moped around all day.

That night, after they had prayed extra hard, Gustie remembered how on one spring Sunday after church, the kind young widow who lived on the hill had admired the locket Gustie's grandmother had given her. Gustie's heart leapt with excitement because she knew the widow was quite wealthy.

Gustie could hardly sleep. She was planning what she would do tomorrow!

When Gustie reached the big door, she timidly knocked. The widow answered the door promptly.

Yes, she remembered Gustie. She often wished she
had ten little girls who were as loving. Her large
beautiful house would not be so silent, so
somber.

When Gustie had finished telling her all about
Wilhelmina, the widow agreed to buy Gustie's
locket and gave her a large gold piece!

Gustie was ecstatic! She skipped all the way to the butcher's shop and bought the plumpest goose there.

She took her change from the butcher to the mercantile (that's what they called stores) and bought some embroidery floss for mother, some pipe tobacco for father and a carved wooden horse for Karl. Oh, what a lovely Christmas they would have this year!

Mrs. Dubrect looked at her daughter and saw her differently than ever before. She gathered her up in her arms and said, "No, child. How could I be angry with you for all that love?"

The next morning was Christmas. Gustie and Karl scurried down the stairs in their night clothes, to see what was inside their stockings. So many treats! Each stocking contained an apple, an orange, a candy cane, some nuts and a beautiful wooden pencil box – blue for Karl and pink for Gustie. When Gustie reached down into the toe of her stocking she found, to her surprise, her locket!

"How did this get here?" she wondered out loud. Father said, "This morning while it was still dark, I got up to milk the cows. While I was in the barn an elegant coach with two bay horses pulled up to the door. Out stepped Mrs. Wilhelm, the widow who lives on the hill. She gave me the locket and told me about it. Then she said, 'Any little girl who loves so deeply deserves to have her locket back.' She also told me that you had named the goose 'Wilhelmina' which is like her last name 'Wilhelm.' She asked to meet your goose, so I invited her to share Christmas dinner with us after church and she accepted!"

Gustie and Karl jumped up and down with glee! Company for Christmas dinner. And she wants to meet Wilhelmina!!

Afterwards they all sang Christmas carols and drank hot cocoa. From that time on Mrs. Wilhelm was a part of the family, just like Wilhelmina was!

"So that's the story of grandmother's locket," said Mrs. McWebb. "Would you girls like more cookies and milk?"

"No thanks, Aunt Bett. The cookies were good, but the story was better."

"Maia, let's pretend we're Gustie and Karl when we get home. Lacey can be Wilhelmina!"

"Okay. Goodbye Aunt Bett, we love you!"

"Goodbye girls, come back again soon and I'll tell you another one."

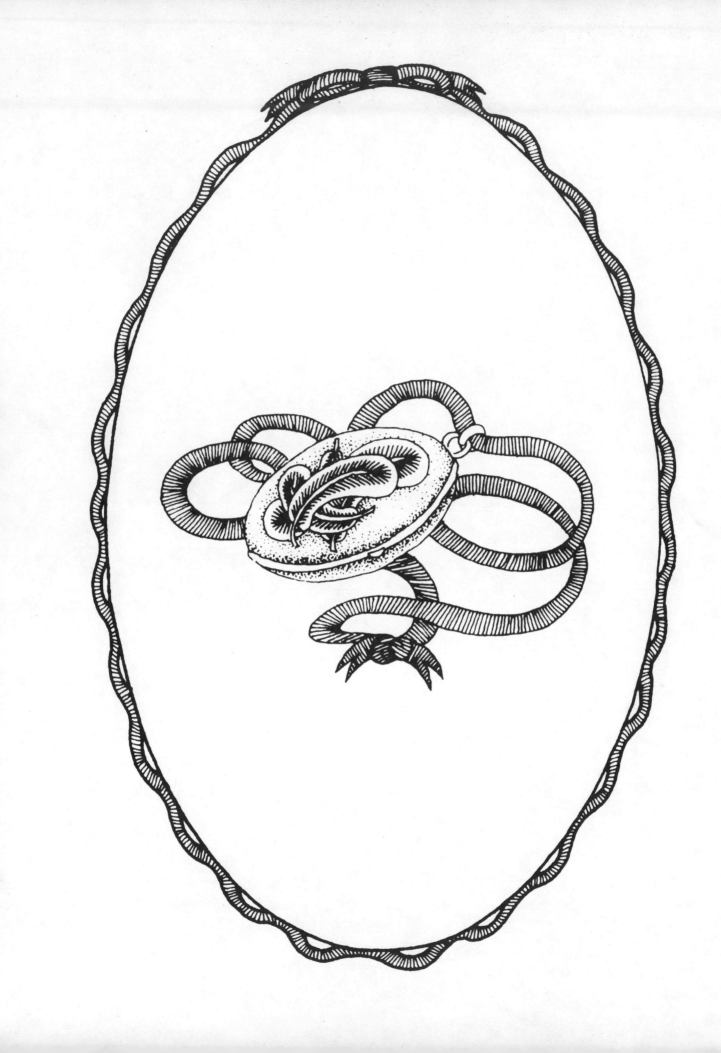